# Loula
## and Mister
### the Monster

To Yasemin, with all my gratitude

Text and illustrations © 2015 Anne Villeneuve

All rights reserved. No part of this publication may be reproduced, stored in a retrieval system or transmitted, in any form or by any means, without the prior written permission of Kids Can Press Ltd. or, in case of photocopying or other reprographic copying, a license from The Canadian Copyright Licensing Agency (Access Copyright). For an Access Copyright license, visit www.accesscopyright.ca or call toll free to 1-800-893-5777.

Kids Can Press acknowledges the financial support of the Government of Ontario, through the Ontario Media Development Corporation's Ontario Book Initiative; the Ontario Arts Council; the Canada Council for the Arts; and the Government of Canada, through the CBF, for our publishing activity.

Published in Canada by
Kids Can Press Ltd.
25 Dockside Drive
Toronto, ON M5A 0B5

Published in the U.S. by
Kids Can Press Ltd.
2250 Military Road
Tonawanda, NY 14150

www.kidscanpress.com

The artwork in this book was rendered in ink and watercolor.
The text is set in Goldenbook.

Edited by Yasemin Uçar
Designed by Karen Powers

This book is smyth sewn casebound.
Manufactured in Shenzhen, China, in 3/2015 through Asia Pacific Offset.

CM 15 0 9 8 7 6 5 4 3 2 1

LIBRARY AND ARCHIVES CANADA CATALOGUING IN PUBLICATION

Villeneuve, Anne, author, illustrator
    Loula and Mister the monster / written and illustrated by Anne Villeneuve.
ISBN 978-1-77138-326-4 (bound)
    I. Title.
PS8593.I3996L66 2015      jC813'.54      C2014-907193-0

Kids Can Press is a **corus**™ Entertainment company

# Loula
## and Mister
### the Monster

Written and illustrated by

# Anne Villeneuve

KIDS CAN PRESS

Everywhere Loula goes, Mister follows.

(Except when it's the other way around.)

Life is splendid, as long as they are together.

But one day, Loula overhears a very troubling conversation ...
"I have had enough!" roars Loula's mother. "I can't live with
that ... that MONSTER anymore!"

Loula has a pretty good idea who her mother is talking about — a certain "monster" who is a little too messy, a little too clumsy and a little too hungry ... a LOT of the time.

That night, Loula is too worried to sleep. She calls a meeting.
"Mister, this is a serious matter. If you don't stop with the bad
manners, Mama will throw you out, like an old pair of shoes!
What would I do without you?"

Loula gives Mister a kiss goodnight. "Don't worry, I'll think of something," she tells him as she drifts off to sleep. "I'm going to turn you into the most perfect little dog no mama can resist."

The next morning, Loula has a plan.

"Wake up, lazybones," she says. "Welcome to Loula's School of Good Manners. LESSON ONE: *Always keep clean and tidy from snout to tail.* Hop in the bath, Mister."

"This tie goes best with your color," says Loula.

"I think this is how Papa does it ..."

"I hope he doesn't mind if I shorten it a little.
I wouldn't want you to trip."

"Very distinguished!" says Loula. "Ready for
LESSON TWO? *Learn the art of table manners.*"

"First, you have to wait until everyone has been served before you start eating the cheese tartines ..."

"Hold your glass with your little finger in the air ..."

Unfortunately, Mister has eyes for only one thing: the cheese tartines!

"Oh, boy," says Loula. "Quick!
Let's get out of here."

Gilbert, the family chauffeur, finds Loula and Mister camped out on the front steps. "Mademoiselle, why so blue?" he asks.

"Oh, Gilbert," replies Loula, "if Mister doesn't learn some good manners fast, Mama will throw him out, like an old pair of shoes! What would I do without him?"

"Did you say good manners?" asks Gilbert. "I have a book about that. It's in one of these pockets ... Ah, here it is."

"What does it say for LESSON THREE?" asks Loula.

"Let me see ... LESSON THREE: *Walk, don't run.* Shall we go to the park, Mademoiselle?"

"That's what I was thinking," says Loula.

"I knew this wouldn't be easy," says Loula,

gripping Mister's leash with all her might.

"Perhaps we should move on to LESSON

FOUR," suggests Gilbert, huffing and puffing.

*"Keep calm and breathe deeply."*

After a relaxing
yoga class in the park,
Mister is finally calm.
"Gilbert, I think
we're ready for the
next lesson."

"LESSON FIVE," says Gilbert, rubbing his back.

*"Stay out of puddles."*

"Good. There are always puddles in the park,"
Loula says. "Let's find one."

"Are you sure this is a good idea, Mademoiselle?
This is an awfully big puddle."

"Yes, Gilbert. If Mister can resist jumping into the
fountain, he can resist any puddle."

Surprisingly, Mister cannot.

"Gilbert," says Loula, "this is harder than
I thought. The lessons don't seem to be working."

"Indeed, Mademoiselle," agrees Gilbert.
"Maybe we should take a break before attempting
LESSON SIX: *Don't jump on everything.*"

Just then, something catches Mister's eye.

"Oh, no! A squirrel!" cries Loula.

"Oh, no! The museum!" cries Gilbert.

"Mister, stop!" Loula yells.

"It's too late," says Gilbert gravely.

"Your dog has failed LESSON SIX."

Loula, Mister and Gilbert are sent straight to
the museum security office.

Then they are sent OUT. And something tells them they won't be invited back to the museum for a long, long time.

"Gilbert, what if my dog is a lost cause?
What if Mama really does send him away?"
"Don't despair, Mademoiselle Loula. A few
more lessons will do the trick ... probably."

"*Shhh,* be very quiet,"
whispers Loula as they
enter the house.

"Where have you been?" exclaims her mother. "It's been
so quiet here without the two of you!"

"Mama, are you going to throw Mister out?" asks Loula.

"Of course not!" her mother replies. "What would we do
without him?"

"Now, please hold the door open for me
so I can throw out this ... this MONSTER."